The Fawn Animal Disguises No Accounting For Tastes Jackets Colder

Sleepy Heads Going Places Animal Jackets "Said the Robin Fawn

Don't Look Like Your Mother," Said the Robin Now That Days Are Colder

Tastes Animal Houses Now That Days Are Colder "You Don't Look

Robin to the Fawn Animal Disguises Filling the Bill Sleepy Heads

Tail Twisters Filling the Bill Sleepy Heads "You Don't Look

Days Are Colder, No Accounting For Tastes Animal Jackets

Sleepy Heads Going Places Animal Jackets Robin to the

"You Don't Look Like Your Mother," Said the Robin

For Tastes Animal Houses Now That Days Are

Animal Jackets Tail Twisters Filling the Bill Sleepy

Said the Robin to the Fawn Animal Disguises You

That Days Are Colder, No Accounting For Tastes

Now That Days Are Colder, No Accounting For

Bill Sleepy Heads Going Places Animal

"You Don't Look Like Your Mother," Said the

Animal Houses Now That Days Are Filling the Bill

Going Places

BOWMAR NATURE SERIES · THE WAYS OF ANIMALS ·

Going Places

by Aileen Fisher

designed and illustrated
by Midge Quenell

lettering by Paul Taylor

bowmar

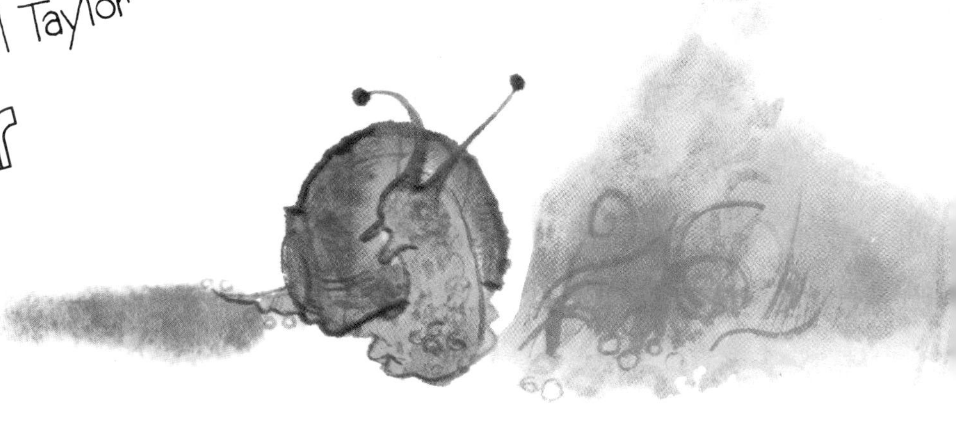

BOWMAR®, Glendale, California 91201.
Manufactured in the United States of America.
International Standard Book Number 0-8372-0865-3.
Library of Congress Catalog Card Number 72-89027.
Distributed in Canada by Thomas Nelson & Sons (Canada) Limited.
Distributed in the United Kingdom by Thomas Nelson & Sons Limited.
United Kingdom edition ISBNo.0-8372-0876-9.

....to Blanche

How do you travel, bird in the sky?

Sometimes I glide,
but mostly I fly.

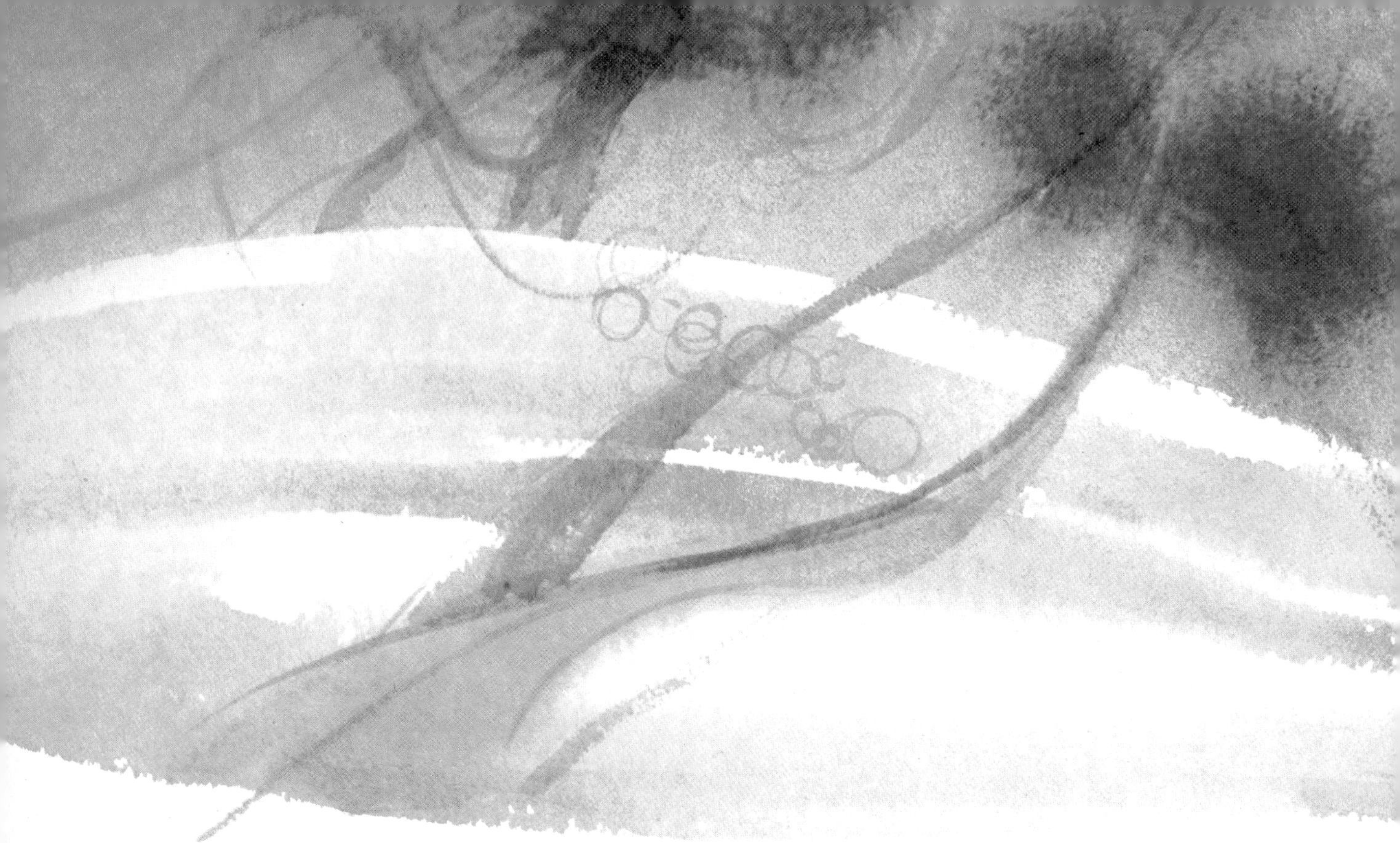

How do you travel, fish in the sea?

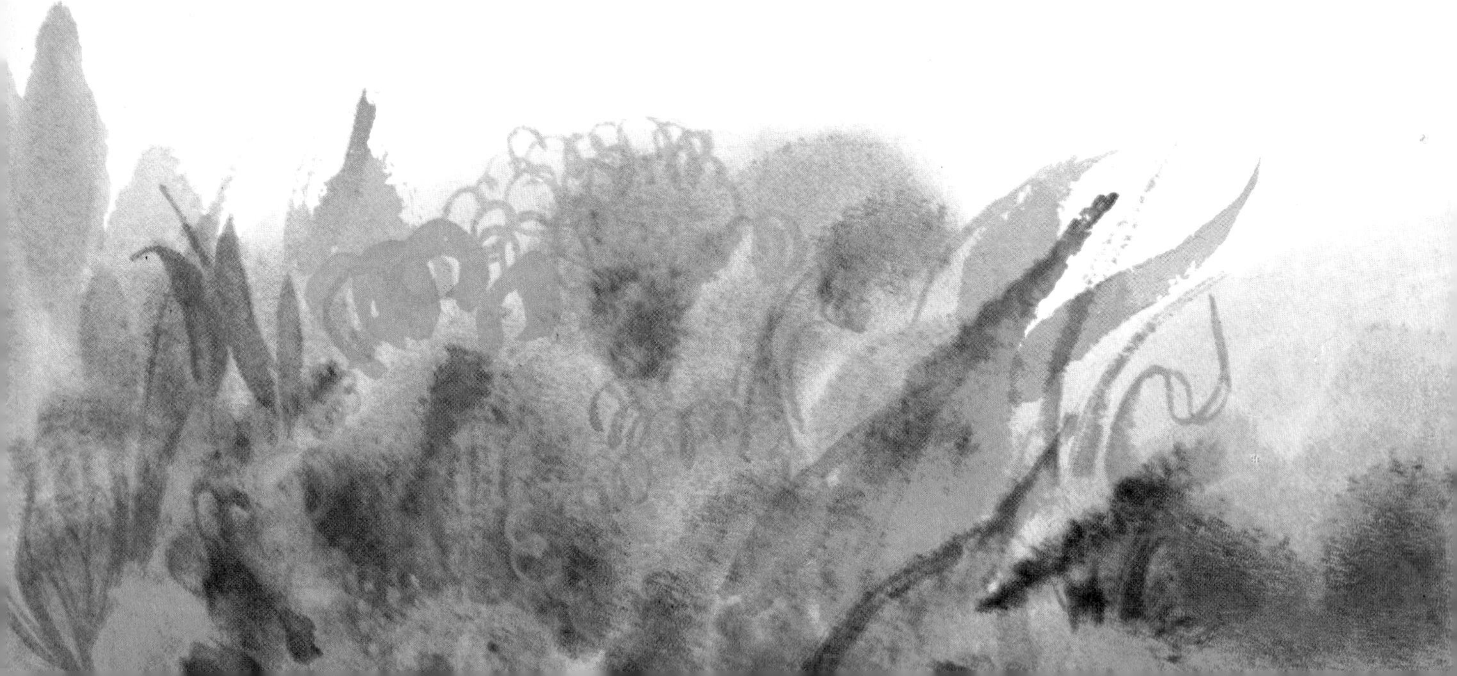

Swimming is always in fashion with me.

How do you travel, slow-moving snail?

My foot muscles move down my own little trail.

I'm not very speedy, but think how you'd be if you had your house on your shoulders —like me.

You, startled rabbit,
what way do YOU go?

By leaps and by bounds over clover and snow.

How do you travel, snake in the grass?

I slither from sight

when passersby pass.

And you, bees and beetles,
and hornets with stings?

We walk on our feet
or fly with our wings

– or jump! said the cricket, as if we had springs.

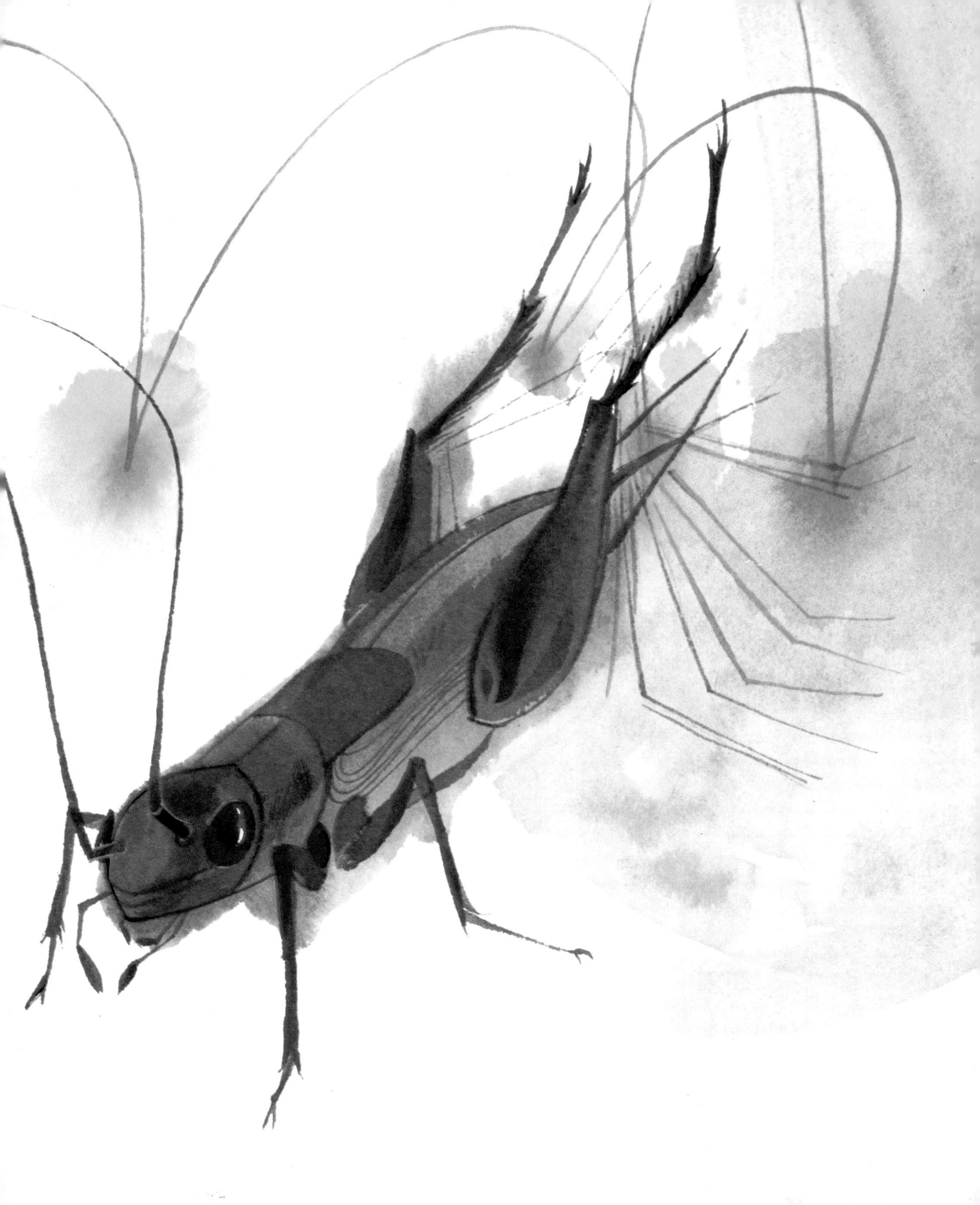

And you, little mouse
in the weeds and the hay?

I run very fast — when I'm running away.

How do you travel, croaky old frog?

I swim in the pond
or leap through the bog.

And you,
small koala,
what is your tack?
I cling to my mother
and ride
pickaback.

And so, said the
baby opossums,
do we.

We cling to our mother
and travel – for free.

And you,
Mr. Penguin,
tailored and trim?

My wings cannot fly, so I walk
and I swim.

How do YOU travel, schoolboy and girl?

We walk and we run.

We skip...........

. . . . and we whirl

We travel by car,

by boat or by plane,

by trolley or bus,

by bike or by train.

And sometime,
though probably not very soon,
we'll purchase a ticket
and go to the moon.